ANIMALS SAV

GN00984139

Part 1

NO MORE PLASTIC

Zac Pepper & Michael Ashby

Advisers:
Issy, Ben, Max, Jamie & Alex

Esplanade Publishing Ltd.
C/O Easterbrook Eaton Ltd. Cosmopolitan house, Old Fore Street,
Sidmouth, Devon EX10 8LS

Cover Design: Antony Cox ac4designs.co.uk

ISBN:
ISBN-9781691380053

CONTENTS

CHAPTER 1

Where's Grandpa?

Jump the squirrel monkey slowly opened his sleepy eyes before stretching out his arms and tail.

Oh no! The sun was shining. His alarm clock, a giant cockerel called Doodle Doo was snoring loudly by his feet. Jump gave the cockerel a kick, but Doodle Doo just rolled over and snored louder than ever. Jump shook his head in despair. He'd have to find a new alarm clock when he got back from his quest. Cockerels were supposed to crow at daybreak, when the sun started to rise. No time for breakfast now. Grabbing his backpack, Jump ran off to try and catch his friends up.

Dung crossed the road
On the back of a slippery toad
When he got to the other side
He said "Thank you Toady for the ride."

Toady looked very carefully at the young dung beetle. He knew that dung beetles were the strongest animals in the whole, wide world for their body size. They could move a ball of poo over 1,000, yes, one thousand times heavier than themselves! They ate poo for breakfast, lunch and dinner.

Amazing! Although why anyone would ever want to eat poo for breakfast, yuk; lunch, yuk yuk; and dinner, yuk yuk yuk, was a complete mystery to Toady.

"Where are you off to Dung? If you don't mind me asking," Toady enquired.

"I'm off to save the world, Toady," Dung replied, with a very determined look on his face.

"Well, it really does need saving, Dung. The human's have mucked it up for all of us. I've never known weather as hot as last summer. It got harder and harder to find a really nice slimy pond to cool off in."

Yuk, thought Dung. He didn't like the sound of a jumping into a slimy pond at all. He preferred the clear water of the local stream where his mum made him have a bath on his birthday.

"Whoa! That's a big job Dung. How are you going to save the world all by yourself?"
Dung smiled.

"Oh, Toady! I won't be all by myself! I'm off to join animals from all over the world!"

"Wow Dung! That's wonderful! Where on Earth are you meeting them all?"

"The Amazon rain forest, Toady."

"Wow! Super Wow! Wowser!" Toady started hopping about in excitement. There were lots of slimy pools and rivers in the Amazon.

"Can I hop along with you Dung and help in your quest to save our world? Please."

"Of course you can, Toady. Welcome aboard team animal!" Too late! Toady remembered the piranha; those razor toothed fish that lived in South America. Perhaps they were friendlier to toads.

"How did your quest start, Dung?"
"Well, Toady, it's a long story. It all began when …"

Yesterday, at breakfast time, Dung's family were all sitting quietly munching their fresh, breakfast rhino poo. Yummy! Dung's youngest sister slowly looked around at everyone eating before squeaking out "Where's andpa?"

She hadn't yet learnt to say gr. Everyone looked up from the large, flat stone they were eating on and looked at the space where grandpa, or andpa, should have been.

"Oh no! Not again!" granny shouted. Grandpa was always forgetting the time. Getting older had made him lose his appetite a bit.

"First things first!" said granny.
"Let's finish breakfast and then we'll all find Captain Grumpy Pants!"

Everyone laughed. Granny gently rolled grandpa's warm ball of rhino poo across the stone, and they all helped themselves to extras as it rolled on by. She knew grandpa wouldn't eat cold poo.

"Over here! Over here!" Dung cried. He'd found his grandpa by the stream.

"Goodness me!" exclaimed granny.

Whoa! Grandpa's in trouble when he get's home, Dung thought to himself.

Grandpa was waving at them all, with a wide grin on his face. He was stumbling around in a large, clear plastic container that he'd managed to squeeze himself into.

"What's that smell granny?" Dung asked, as he sniffed the small mouth of the container. Granny sniffed it too.

"Oh no! Dung. It's fermented apple juice that's called cider. Grandpa must have swallowed some, and it's made him all tiddley."

They all watched as grandpa rolled over and waved his legs in the air. He had a huge grin on his face. Granny had seen enough; but she really wished she hadn't.

"Drag the bottle back home, Dung. We'll try and get him out so I can put grandpa on the naughty stone. Again!"

Soon home, they all surrounded the bottle and waited for granny to tell them what to do. Granny always knew what to do when someone needed help.

"Right. Lift up the bottom of the bottle."

They all grinned as a snoring grandpa slid down the bottle towards the small entrance where he'd squeezed in.

"Push the bottle into the elephant enclosure and ask Billy to carefully stand on the bottom of the bottle."

Dung first pushed the bottle under a huge gate before crawling up the front leg of a baby elephant. He whispered into one of its' enormous, flappy ears. Billy nodded before gently bringing one of his feet carefully down on the back of the plastic bottle. They all heard a whoosh of escaping air, which carried a snoring grandpa along with it. He shot out of the plastic container's mouth and safely landed on a small pile of hay. Grandpa sat up slowly, awake again, and shouted out "Breakfast time!"

Granny tried to look serious but even she eventually joined in laughing.

CHAPTER 2

Feather Flight

Dung and Toady eventually reached their local airport set in a nearby nature reserve. This was their first visit and they were amazed at how busy it was. Animals of many species were arriving and departing for all over the country. Some lucky ones were going even further.

Two parrots appeared and landed right in front of a very startled Dung and Toady. "Dong!" shouted the first parrot.

"Ding!" shouted the other parrot, who then looked most annoyed at her twin sister.

"Hey!" she complained. "It's my turn to go first today!"

"Sorry, Petunia. I forgot. Can we start again pleease?"
Dung and Toady looked on, completely mystified.

"Ding!"

"Dong!"

"Welcome to Feather Airways. This is the flight announcement for all passengers departing for the Amazon rain forest today. Please make your way now to our tallest take off tree. We hope you enjoy travelling with Feather Airways. Have a safe flight."

Petunia looked at her sister. They had said each word together, in time. Smiling at their two customers they flew off to greet their next arrivals.

Toady looked at Dung.

"How did they know we were going to the Amazon, Dung?"

"Good question Toady. I got my rat friend, Pickles, to book a couple of seats on the Animal Net. Before you ask, Toady, think of all the smartphones that human's lose every day;

like, leaving them on a car roof while looking for their keys and then driving off! Silly Billys! Well, any animal that finds one takes it to their local rat network. It's a long story Toady, but, together with centipedes' magical code cracking feet, the rats have set up a global Animal communication network right under the humans' noses!"

"Whoa Dung! That's *way* too hard for me!" replied Toady, shaking his head.

"I'll stick to mud and slimy ponds Dung! You do the clever

stuff! Now, where's that big tree. They all look big to me!"

"Hurry up! Hurry up! You're going to miss your flight!" the grey squirrel shouted at them. They'd found their tree at last. Looking up, it seemed to disappear into the very clouds that they would soon be flying through. Speedy the squirrel looked at Toady and grabbed a clump of moss.

"Sorry about this Toady, but you're a bit too slippery for flying. We don't want you slipping off while you're airborne, do we?"

Toady kept obediently still as Speedy wiped his slimiest bits off.

"That's better, Toady!" Toady wasn't too sure about that.

"You climb up on my back, Toady; and Dung, you climb up my front leg and settle in under Toady's comfy chin. Human's use lifts or elevators to climb up tall buildings. So look upon me as your lift to our Amazon flight departure branch. Hang on tight Toady! Snuggle in Dung!"

Speedy took off up the tree like a rocket. In fact, Rocket was his second name!

Toady and Dung just about held on. Half way up Toady whispered to Dung "Do you think any animal has ever fallen off Speedy?"

"That's not a very helpful question right now, Toady!" Dung replied nervously. Speedy had heard Toady's worried voice and he smiled to himself. Speedy knew that Grabber, a Peregrine falcon was safely watching over them. Any falling passengers would be caught in an instant by Grabber's safe claws, before being delivered in a rather shocked state to their departure branch. The last animal Grabber had saved was a slippery eel whose knot around Speedy's tummy had come undone.

Dung bravely opened his eyes and was amazed at how high Speedy had already climbed. "Wow!" he cried in excitement. His quest had started.

Just a couple of heart beats later, Speedy stopped. They carefully climbed off Speedy who, after wishing them a safe flight, soared through the air to land safely on one of the lower branches.

Dung and Toady were so high in the sky that they both edged slowly backwards to feel the reassurance of the solid tree trunk. Neither could talk. The view in front of them really was breathtaking and so beautiful. Dung suddenly realized that this view was what it was all about. Trying to save our magnificent planet earth. Dung looked across the woods and fields to the twinkling river with rising hills beyond. His quest must not fail.

A deep, wise voice brought Dung back to Feather Flight.

"Hellooo!"

Dung and Toady carefully turned round and looked up. "Welcome to your Feather Flight departure branch. I'm Snowball the snowy owl. I've popped across from the Arctic for a few days to help out since Feather Flight is going to be very busy."

Dung and Toady looked up in amazement. There was a hole in the tree trunk, and they could see Snowball peering out at them.

"Your Feather Flight today is a golden eagle. My, my, aren't you the lucky ones! Your pilot and Feather Flight is Captain McGreedy. Now, listen carefully. I hope you both already know that we have to activate your micro-animal button just before you board McGreedy. Obviously, McGreedy wouldn't be best pleased if a grown up elephant sat down on him and said fly me to Africa. So, Speedy's sister will push your micro button just as you board McGreedy. Any questions? No. Wonderful! I can go back to sleep now. Just walk out along the branch. Toodle-oo woo."

McGreedy turned his head to check out the passengers. He noticed there was just one empty seat. Cuckoo, the airport controller flew past.

"Five second countdown McGreedy. A safe flight to you all."

McGreedy nodded and started counting down.

"Five!"

Dung looked in despair at the empty seat. Where had Jump

got to? He was normally so punctual.

At that moment Jump was living up to his name and jumping over Ding and Dong, who together had told him that it was too late to board his flight. The tree was closed.

"Four!"

Jump started climbing the tree as quickly as he could.

"Three!"

Goodness! This was such a tall tree. Jump looked up and reckoned he was already halfway up.

"Two!"

Jump speeded up. There was the take-off branch!

"One!"

Jump was halfway along the take-off branch and he could see McGreedy spreading his wings.

"Lift Off!"

McGreedy's talons released their grip on the branch and he was airborne. Jump raced along the branch.

Dung and Toady looked back. They could see Jump racing along the take-off branch towards them. All the passengers had turned their heads too and were chanting "Jump! Jump! Jump!" Jump jumped into the air after them.

"Oh no!" Dung and Toady thought. Jump was still the proper size! Then they saw a peregrine falcon swoop down in a flash and push Jump's micro-animal button and next moment a much smaller Jump magically landed in his seat right next to Dung and Toady.

McGreedy casually turned his head to look at Jump.

"Thank you so much for dropping in Mr. Jump. Snacks will be served shortly."

CHAPTER 3

Operation Flying Poo

After the Animal Council meeting deep in the Amazon rain forest, the animals all returned home to prepare for operation 'NO MORE PLASTIC'.

They had decided to take action in one week's time on Christmas Eve. That was the day a lot of working humans started their Christmas holidays.

The last piece of the Animal Council's plan was keeping many red rock crabs and a rough-toothed dolphin called Chewy very busy indeed. They lived on a part of the Namibia coast in West Africa. This length of coastline was heavily guarded by humans because on the sand and seabed were many small stones. They were gemstones called diamonds; and they were worth a lot of money.

Nipper the red rock crab carefully placed the large, dull white diamond he had found into Chewy's wide open mouth. He scuttled off quickly because there was a long line of crabs behind him waiting with their valuable diamonds of all different colours.

Jump, Toady and Dung returned home to a hero's welcome party. Most animals present hadn't been abroad before, and they wanted to hear all about Feather Flight, the giant Amazon river and the rainforest. However, there was no time to chat. There was so much to be organized before Christmas Eve.

The World Plastics Factory was huge. It was set all alone, surrounded by farmland, forest and the sea. The factory had railway lines, a port and a giant road. Supplies to produce plastic arrived all the time, and plastic products were sent out around the globe.

The factory only closed down once a year on Christmas Eve, and reopened again after New Year's Day. A large team of maintenance men always went into the factory on Christmas Day.

Animals started arriving on Christmas Eve morning for operation 'NO MORE PLASTIC'. They all stayed carefully out of sight of the humans. Jump, Dung and Toady had been the first to arrive with their new anaconda friend, Abby. Abby was one of the largest snakes in the world.

The factory shut at lunchtime, and it's manager, Mr. Rich was the first to leave in his posh, shiny, chauffer driven car.

"It's starting to empty," whispered Dung to his friends. They were watching from a large fir tree overlooking the factory's entrance.

Then coaches started streaming out and roaring away, all full of happy, singing workers wearing colourful paper hats. Finally, four big security guards could be seen checking that doors were locked before one of them pressed a remote key in his hand and the gigantic gates started to roll shut. Just as he was placing the remote key back in his pocket, two large, fierce sea gulls dive bombed him and pinched an open bag of crisps from his other hand. He frantically waved them away, angrily shouting and pointing "The sea's that way! It's full of real fish! Go and catch some, you lazy daisies!"

He was so annoyed that he didn't see the raccoon twins roll quietly out from under his van. Nor did he see them pick up his remote key that he had dropped. The raccoons tiptoed away quietly towards the safety of the trees, their grey coats blending in with the road. The natural black masks around their eyes made them look like the robbers you see in cartoon films.

Satisfied all was safe, the four security men waved at a camera set on top of a tall concrete post, before climbing into their van and driving off for the Christmas holidays.

"Wow! Dung. The plan's just about to start."
Jump screeched in excitement.

Dung suddenly looked serious. There was an awful lot that could go wrong.

"Calm down! Jump. Give Billy the order to launch operation FLYING POO!"

Twenty five miles away on a deserted industrial estate, one building still had a human in it. Since Noelle wasn't married, she had volunteered to work on Christmas Eve. She sat comfortably in her chair watching lots of small TV screens while munching a large tub of popcorn. Noelle worked for the security company that monitored the cameras keeping the World Plastics Factory safe.

She waved at the screen showing the four security guards driving off.

"Merry Christmas," she said, before closing her eyes for a few seconds to concentrate on munching a Christmas sized mouthful of popcorn. Yummy!

Back at The World Plastics Factory, giant flocks of birds had been flying in all morning. There were fifty species in total, from all around the world. They included American bald eagles, Vultures, California Condors, Arctic terns, West Indian whistling ducks, hummingbirds and albatrosses.

Each species had been given a different area to hide in around the huge factory, and were placed near one of the concrete pole cameras. As soon as they heard Billy the elephant roar trumpety trump! all the birds took off.

The massive golden eagles led the attack on the camera by the main gate. Since the security cameras had a bird's eye view - they could see in all directions - the golden eagles split into four groups. Group 1 flew in from the south led by McGreedy, a fearsome bird that had been eating extra haggis, Scotland's national dish, especially for today's important mission.

McGreedy flew in slightly higher than the concrete pole. Sensing that now was the right time for operation FLYING POO he released a giant poo bomb from his bahooky, a Scottish word for bum! It flew through the air to land splat! right on the camera. Result!

When the other golden eagle groups from the north, east and west had done their business too, the top of the concrete pole was in a sorry state. No camera could be seen as it was completely covered in golden eagle poo. McGreedy glanced across to the next two cameras and was pleased to see that the white tailed eagles and the sparrow hawks had been spot on with their flying poo bombs.

Back in Noelle's control room a screen had gone dark. Underneath it a small sign said 'Main Gate'. Noelle didn't notice because she had fallen into a deep sleep. Her arms had relaxed which sadly meant that her beloved tub of popcorn had fallen onto the floor scattering popcorn everywhere.

McGreedy landed on the grass right in front of the trees in which Jump and his team were hiding.

"Okay, everyone! It's safe to come out now!"
Jump peeped his head out from behind a tree trunk.

"Are you absolutely sure McGreedy?"

"Completely sure, Jump. I've flown two laps right round the factory and all the cameras are completely plastered and covered over!"

Jump walked out into the open and turned to Billy.

"Sound the all clear, Billy!" Billy the baby elephant took a large, deep breath before letting out two gigantic trumpety trumps that left him a bit red in the face. All the animals that had been hiding, crept carefully out of the woods.

Goodness! They were really taking part in something very special. If all went well, they would have a wonderful story to tell their family and friends when they returned home.

Jump screeched loudly and the chattering around him stopped.

"Okay! First off, McGreedy." The golden eagle flapped his wings excitedly and Dung would have blown away had not Toady held him down with an extra slimy front foot.
Yuk! But thanks, Toady.

"Well done McGreedy! Please congratulate all the birds that took part. Now, I have a little treat for you McGreedy! Please calm your wings down first!" McGreedy folded his wings.

"Billy! McGreedy's present please!"

Billy stuck his trunk behind a tree and brought out a dark, large ball.

"Your favourite award winning haggis from Renfrewshire!"

Tears rolled from McGreedy's eyes.

"Thank you Jump. I'll share it with all my teams. A tiny taste of home!"

Jump looked at his two most trusted friends. A red fox called Copper and a white tailed deer called Thorns.

"Time for operation POO DUMP Copper. Get the raccoon twins to open the main gates and then organize the elephants' operation FLATTEN!"
 Copper raced off. Jump turned to look at Thorns.
  "Right Thorns; get your three teams to prepare for all our deliveries by road, rail and sea. Last I heard, everyone's going to be arriving on time. The most important job is to get the orangutans delivering and rolling the gravel behind the elephant army. No go karting antics please! The giraffes can

make sure they stick to the plan."

Thorns leapt off. So much to do. So little time to do it in.

Jump turned to Billy and raced up his trunk, which Billy had just lowered to the ground.

"Okay, Billy. Let's see if we can get all the security lights pointing outwards towards the woods, so that Team Animal can work right through the night." Billy trumpeted and set off towards the main gates that the black masked raccoon twins had just opened.

"Well done! Great start you two! Thank the seagulls for me."
"Thanks, Jump! Will do."

Jump was through the main gates now, and suddenly he realized it was all going too well.
Could their good luck last?

Back at the control centre Noelle had just woken up. She yawned, stretched and rubbed her eyes. Oh no! She'd dropped her popcorn.
Noelle suddenly realized the control room was a little darker.

The TV monitor screens were all black! What on earth was going on at the World Plastics Factory on Christmas Eve? Perhaps there had been a power failure. This was serious. She pushed a button on the microphone in front of her.

On the roof of Noelle's building a young silver back gorilla answered his smartphone.

"She's awake! Start the jammer."

"Thanks dormouse! I'm on it." From a tiny hole in the control room wall a dormouse clicked her phone off.

Bananas looked down at his tech support rat.
"Time to test the jammer! Ring your granny and then I'll switch the jammer on."

Back in the control room Noelle couldn't understand why the microphone wasn't working. She couldn't get through to mobile security.
If she could have seen the state of the radio aerial on the roof after Bananas had twisted it into a right old mess, she would have caught on.

Oh well. I'll try to alert the police on the landline.

Noelle picked up the phone, but was surprised to find it was dead. She didn't hear the laughing dormouse who had chewed through the phone line in seconds. She'd have to use her own mobile. Where was it?

"Granny it's me! Merry Chris ... Hey! Bananas. You cut me off! I was talking to my Granny!"

"The jammer's working! Quick! To the lookout!"

Both animals rushed to the front of the roof and carefully peered over. Noelle's little yellow car had been gently moved by three rhinos. It was now completely blocking the front door to the control centre. Just as well Noelle had a freezer full of pizzas and a microwave in the control room.

CHAPTER 4

Christmas Day

Mr. Grumpy was in charge of maintenance at the World Plastics Factory. He sat in the front row behind his coach driver. A crocodile of five coaches, full of unhappy maintenance workers, were three miles away from the factory. Despite getting paid extra wages for working on a bank holiday they would all prefer to have been back home. Mr. Grumpy sniffed the air.

"Can you smell anything Fred?" he asked the driver. Fred coughed.

"What's that awful stink!" Fred shouted in reply, as he quickly checked the coach's air conditioning controls.

Turning in his seat and seeing rows of workers starting to cough and hold handkerchiefs and scarves to cover their noses, Mr. Grumpy decided that this awful pong wasn't caused by just one or two nasty bottom burps. It smelt to him like a sewage works. Hopefully it would all blow away soon.

The crocodile of coaches turned the last corner about one mile away from the main gates. The smell hadn't blown away. Mr. Grumpy was now becoming worried that something had gone seriously wrong at the factory, and that some chemicals had leaked and mixed together to make this smell.

Was it dangerous? Should they all turn round?

It was his responsibility to keep these workers and drivers safe.

Suddenly, Fred braked hard and their coach screeched to a

halt. Mr. Grumpy was about to find out that his bad start to Christmas day was about to get worse. Much worse. Much, much worse.

Fred and Mr. Grumpy couldn't believe their eyes.
Were they dreaming?
Mr. Grumpy rubbed his eyes, before pinching his leg hard.
Ouch! No! He wasn't dreaming.
The giant road ahead was completely blocked.
Two huge policemen were shining torches from side to side in warning.

"Open the doors, Fred. I'll go and see what the holdup is." Fred opened the passenger door and the smell that blew in nearly took their breath away. Mr. Grumpy noticed Fred quickly close the coach door behind him as he climbed off the coach.

As Mr. Grumpy approached the two giant policemen, he suddenly noticed they were rather hairy. Too hairy, in fact! They had hairy faces, hairy hands and hairy feet!

Oh no! They were two, large brown bears; each wearing blue

trousers, yellow safety jackets and blue caps.

Mr. Grumpy wiped his streaming eyes with a hanky. Beyond these two bears the huge road was covered in sleeping animals.

Good grief! They were all sloths! His daughter's favourite stuffed toy. These definitely weren't stuffed. They were snoring, burping, drooling, twitching and scratching. There must be hundreds of them, stretching all the way back to the factory gates.

The factory gates! He couldn't see the factory gates! There was a giant hill of ... oh no! It looked like poo! It must be the height of five Mr. Grumpys standing on each other's heads! Worse than that, from what he could see, the giant poo hill went off both to the left and right of the gates, as if to cut off the factory. What was going on?

Mr. Grumpy turned and ran back to the coach, hoping and praying that the bears wouldn't chase or indeed eat him for their Christmas lunch. Oh no! They might pull him apart like a

Christmas cracker, hoping that a present and a paper hat would drop out.

Fred opened the coach door but, before he could ask what was going on, a panicky Mr. Grumpy was dialing 999 on his phone and asking for the police.

"What's the nature of your emergency sir?"

"There's two giant bears dressed as policemen waving torches! The road's blocked with hundreds of sleeping sloths! Behind them there's a giant wall of poo! Help!"

"A merry Christmas to you too, Sir. Did you pinch some of Santa's sherry? What time did you start drinking this morning?"

The police operator sighed. Of all the hoax calls she had ever answered, this one really took Rudolf the reindeer's Christmas biscuit!

Mr. Grumpy screamed before passing the phone to Fred.

High in a nearby tree, Jump, Toady and Dung heard Mr. Grumpy scream. Jump smiled.

Their plan might actually work after all!

Right. Onto the next part.

"Well team! That went well, time to launch the camera drone and let the whole world see what's going on here." Jump pressed a button on a small panel balanced on his lap before grabbing the two small control levers sticking out of it.

"Five, four, three, two, one. Lift off!"

All three animals peered over the branch to the ground below and saw the small camera drone rise slowly into the air.

Jump flew the camera drone back to beyond the last coach, before raising it higher into the air and gently turning it around to face towards the World Plastics Factory.

"Picture quality?" Jump asked, before risking a quick look up. All the branches around him were full of rats on their smartphones, streaming the drone camera's pictures to news organizations all over the world. They all smiled at Jump, hardly believing that after all the hard work last night, the fun part was now underway.

"Great! Time for a close up on the front coach, the bears and the sloths. Turn the dial up a little, camera team."

Toady and Dung slowly moved the camera's zoom control that they were in charge of.

Mr. Rich, the World Plastics Factory manager, was spending Christmas at his huge country mansion. It had fifteen bedrooms and twenty toilets. Mr. Rich had no wife or children because he loved money far too much to love anyone else. He was looked after by his elderly mother. Mr. Rich was far too mean to employ a housekeeper to help her or indeed pay a gardener to mow his lawns. He liked keeping his mother busy. Pity his mother was losing her sight then he wouldn't have had to waste money paying for a chauffeur.

Sitting alone in his huge dining room at the head of a table that could seat twenty people, he was just about to start eating his enormous Christmas morning breakfast cooked, as usual, by his mother. Three fried eggs, two huge sausages, four rashers of bacon, two pieces of fried bread, mushrooms, tomatoes and a hill of baked beans. Oh no! His mother had forgotten the tomato ketchup. She really would have to try harder if she expected to keep enjoying living with him for free.

"Mother! You've forgotten my ketchup again!" he roared. The dining room door slowly opened and his mother stuck her head round.

"I think you should turn the telly on, dear," she whispered in a rather frightened voice, before disappearing. Something about his mother's voice made him put down his knife and fork before reaching for the television control. No tomato ketchup was about to be the least of his problems for now.

"These pictures are being streamed live from above the road into the World Plastics Factory. As you can clearly see, the five maintenance coaches are trapped from behind by an army of vans from global TV and other media organizations …"

Mr. Rich sat frozen in shock.

He was already quite cold since he was far too mean to put the heating on.

" ... blocking the road ahead is the simply incredible sight of an army of sleeping sloths."

The camera moved quickly above the sloths and stopped at the factory entrance

"Here is a giant mountain of some sort of pooey looking material ..."

The picture displayed a higher aerial scene, and the huge hill of poo could be seen cutting the entire factory off.

The TV commentator was sounding far too excited for Mr. Rich's liking.

"Reports from the scene are of a horrific, sewage works smell throughout the area; and some lucky reporters are wearing face masks."

Mr. Rich's phones started ringing. He smashed them all in a fury against his dining room wall.

" ... and now we go to our business correspondent back in the news room."

"Analysts are all saying they expect the value of the World

Plastics Company to fall sharply. Quite simply, this is a media nightmare for them …".

Mr. Rich screamed. Had he looked out of the window he would have seen a taxi leaving down his huge drive.

His mother had had enough. She was off to live with her sister. She asked the driver to wait a minute at the end of the long drive where a life size statue of Mr. Rich greeted, or frightened off visitors at the entrance to his estate. Climbing from the taxi she rummaged in her large handbag.

Taking aim at her son's cold face she started laughing and squeezing as hard as she could.

"Forgotten your tomato ketchup, have I? I think not!"

Mr. Grumpy noticed that the two bears had disappeared.

"Right Fred! I've had enough. It's Mr. Grumpy action time. There's just *so* much work for all of us waiting at the factory." Taking a very deep breath Mr. Grumpy gave Fred the thumbs up and the coach door opened.

If he could just shift one of these sloths the others might

leave. Mr. Grumpy jumped off his coach and ran over to the nearest sloth. Just as Mr. Grumpy reached out his hands to grab the sloth's legs, his phone rang. He recognized the ring tone; it was his young daughter. It must be an emergency for her to ring him at work.

As Mr. Grumpy answered his phone he found that he just couldn't stop coughing, so he put the loudspeaker on.

"DADDY! Don't you dare touch that sloth. It's Haytor! He's a world champion bodyboard surfer. Look up Daddy. You're on TV! If you touch Haytor I'll throw all your underpants out of …"

Mr. Grumpy looked up and saw the camera drone. Oh no! While a global television audience desperately waited to hear what was going to happen to Mr. Grumpy's underpants, things suddenly got even worser for Mr. Grumpy.

"Hello allo! What going on here then?" Police Constable Pudding put his huge hand on Mr. Grumpy's shoulder.

"If you touch that sloth, sir, I'll arrest you for attacking an endangered wild animal."

Mr. Grumpy turned in shock. He hadn't heard the policeman approach. Haytor opened an eye and winked at the policeman. PC Pudding sought to reassure the sloth.

"Just you go back to sleep, Mr. Sloth. I'll deal with this troublemaker."

Leading Mr. Grumpy back to his coach the policeman explained.

"Look Mr. Grumpy; these harmless animals have to be

protected. Millions are watching us on TV and their phones at this very moment. Didn't you know that humans care more about animals than other humans? Especially sleeping sloths!"

Haytor let out an enormous bottom burp as a very sheepish Mr. Grumpy was led back to his coach.

CHAPTER 5

Christmas Animal Magic

Jump was getting very worried now. He kept moving restlessly along the branch, backwards and forwards, much to the increasing irritation of all the other animals sharing his branch.

Only he and the Amazon Animal Council knew all the different parts of the plan that was now in motion. Would it work? Could animals really bring about change of this importance to protect our planet?

Calm down Jump! He thought back to Grandpa Dung getting stuck in a large plastic container and all that had happened since then.

Well, at least they'd tried.

Lost in his thoughts he didn't notice McGreedy landing right by him until two familiar voices, Dung and Toady, shouted together

"It worked! Jump. It really worked!"

Thirty minutes ago.

The head of The World Animal Bank, Coin, lived alone on an island. This island was set in the middle of a lake, amidst a huge safari park.

In his house he had a large TV screen that his most trusted human friend, Mary his keeper, had connected to the internet for him. Just before Christmas, Coin, a huge silverback gorilla had got Mary to contact the most important companies who owned large chunks of The World Plastics Factory.

The World Animal Bank was offering to buy their chunks at

half their current value. This offer would only last until lunchtime on Christmas day. Obviously, none had taken Coin up on his very cheeky offer.

However, with the World Plastics Factory now cut off from the world and billions of people around the globe watching it live streaming on their TVs and smartphones, it came as no surprise to Coin that Mary's phone suddenly started ringing. Scared people suddenly wanted to sell their chunks of The World Plastics Factory.

The red rock crabs that had found diamonds on a West African beach; the turtles that found golden pirate treasures beneath the sand in the Caribbean; octopuses that pulled priceless objects from long ago sunken Spanish galleons; oysters who gave up their perfect pearls; grizzly bears who found gold in mountain streams.

All these riches and countless more that lay beyond the reach of humans, but were accessible to animals, made the World Animal Bank the richest and most secretive in the world; with the help of just a few trusted humans of course.

Remember, over two thirds of planet earth is covered in water. Just think of all the natural riches hidden by the sea.

Mary finally put her phone down, and looked at Coin. He gave her the thumbs up. Mary whooped! Coin raised a hand in celebration, but Mary knew from experience that you really don't want to high five a large, silverback gorilla!

Coin carefully put his keyboard down. He'd

transferred a lot of money this morning. He flapped his arms like a bird and Dung and Toady got the message. Thanking Jane and Coin they rushed outside where McGreedy was waiting. Time to let Jump know the best news ever!

Jump breathed a huge sigh of relief.

It had worked! No more plastic would be made at this factory ever again. A warning had been sent out around the world by the animal kingdom. Time now to work some

Christmas animal magic before the hard work began to convert the factory to sustainable and environmentally friendly packaging.

So much to do!

Jump waved a pretend magic wand.

The skunks hiding behind the first row of trees near the maintenance coaches and news crews heard Billy the baby elephant give the magic signal.

"Trumpety Trump! Trumpety Trump!"

The skunks all stopped spraying the strong stinky smell from their bottoms and slowly made their way into the woods to catch Feather Flights home to North and South America.

The stink birds from the Amazon rain forest watched on with their new flamingo friends, as the large heaps of sperm whale poo, which they'd all been adding to, were carefully pushed by reversing rhino bums into large holes; before being covered over with soil and trampled down by Billy's family and friends.

Slowly, the smell in the air breathed in by the maintenance men and reporters started to improve. After a cloud of birds had dropped dried lavender, thyme and rosemary with their wonderful soothing smells, Mr. Grumpy first noticed that his eyes had stopped watering, and then that the coughing in the coach had stopped. He looked at Fred the driver and asked him "Do you think we should risk it?"

Fred nodded in agreement and opened the coach door. A refreshing smell of herbs blew in and almost brought a smile to Mr. Grumpy's face. What on earth was going on?

Mr. Grumpy and Fred both wanted to know.

Jump knew exactly what was going on. Time now to use the magician's greatest secret weapon.

Distraction.

Make the humans look one way while the magic trick is prepared!

Jump screeched with excitement. Oh! Please, please work, Christmas animal magic.

Fred noticed them first and quickly pressed the button that closed the coach door.

Was he dreaming?

He looked at Mr. Grumpy for reassurance that he wasn't going completely bonkers. Seeing Mr. Grumpy's wide open mouth and shocked expression, and hearing gasps of astonishment from the maintenance workers sitting behind him, he realized that he really wasn't dreaming.

In the front news van a lady reporter was talking to a TV camera.

"In the last few minutes the terrible sewage-like smell has eased off, and as you can see I've even opened our van window a little. The incredible events unfolding outside the World Plastics factory has certainly taken the world by storm. Social media is reporting that children from all over the world are asking their parents to bring them here today so that they can show their support for the brave sloths who are stopping maintenance, and eventually, plastic production.

Goodness me! What's that noise? Help!"

A giant herd of elephants led by Billy had come out of the trees by the coaches and news vans. The biggest of them was Billy's dad and he stood right in front of Mr. Grumpy's maintenance coach completely blocking the view.

Billy had stuck his trunk in through the open window of the front TV van and grabbed what he thought was an ice cream cornet out of the startled lady reporter's hand.

Must be nuts in this, it's very crunchy, Billy thought.

Billy swallowed the microphone which kept broadcasting Billy's gurgling tummy noise to all the watching viewers.

  While the lady reporter screamed with shock, her cameraman kept on filming.

By the end of the day this became the most played video on social media. Billy the baby elephant had made both of them global celebrities.

   Despite Jump having asked the elephants not to cause any damage, Billy's mum had slipped on a banana skin while itching her huge bottom against the small police car. That police car is now much smaller. Fortunately, PC Noel Pudding was having a wee against a tree during that car crushing moment.

After just five minutes of elephant time the sky darkened as a huge cloud of birds flew over. This was the signal to the elephants. Time to go home.

In the front maintenance coach Mr. Grumpy watched as all the elephants disappeared back into the woods. Suddenly, Fred shouted out.

"Look Mr. Grumpy! The roads all clear."

Mr. Grumpy looked ahead.
The sloths were all gone!

"Quick Fred! Start the engine and put your foot down. Perhaps we can catch up on the maintenance work."

Driving towards the main gate Fred and Mr. Grumpy shouted out together.

"The great wall of poo has gone as well!"

Fred asked Mr. Grumpy where it had gone. Mr. Grumpy was a

clever man. He just couldn't understand. Where had it gone and how had it been moved so quickly? Mr Grumpy scratched his head as they approached the factory gates. Just by the gates he could see a huge, covered large thingy with a lady and a small group of animals in front of it. Goodness! That's the baby elephant who had swallowed that lady reporter's microphone. What on earth was going on? He'd be so pleased to just get home this evening, put his slippers on and completely forget about today.

Five minutes earlier, with the coaches and vans surrounded by elephants, Jump turned to one of his most trusted friends, Thorns the fawn.

"Right Thorns. While the humans are all distracted you go and wake the sloths up and send them home. Please thank them for acting asleep! They were very realistic. Their Feather Flights are waiting."

"I think they all fell asleep while they were acting to be asleep, Jump," Thorns replied. They both laughed before

Thorns set off shouting "Wakey, Wakey!"

Jump turned to his other trusted friends, Copper, a red fox and McGreedy.
"Okay you two. Time for our big illusion to end. It's Operation LIFT THE POO time."

No matter what he did, Thorns just couldn't wake Haytor up. He'd tickled the sloth, gently pushed and shouted at him. Thorns looked up at Jump watching on anxiously from his lookout branch.

Suddenly, Thorns saw a bright red fire engine parked on the

edge of the woods near Mr. Grumpys' coach. Jump saw it too and sent Cuddles the orangutan to help Thorns.

Thorns stood by a large hose reel. Cuddles caught on, and started unrolling the hose towards the sleeping sloths. The firemen were nowhere to be seen.

Cuddles stood with the hose ready and looked back at Thorns. Thorns saw a big green button next to the hose reel that he pushed with his nose. Water started snaking through the hose, and Cuddles delighted in waking up the sloths with Thorns newly invented, water squirting, giant red alarm clock! Haytor was dreaming that he was on his bodyboard riding a huge wave onto the beach. Haytor could see the gold cup ahead. He reached out his arm to take it, just as the wave crashed.

Haytor stuck out his tongue and tasted the water. It wasn't salty! He opened his eyes and saw Cuddles aiming a hose right at him! Time to go. The sloths had played their part.

With the sloths now awake and moving off, Cuddles started washing all the skunk stinky away. Skunk pong took an awful lot of washing away!

Jump was now on his way to the factory gates. As planned, the only remaining part of the giant wall of poo stretched across the road in front of the gates. He could see Copper and McGreedy directing two tractors being driven by bears wearing yellow safety jackets.

The green tractor waited at one end of the huge wall while elephants and orangutans connected a chain to it. The animals backed away and watched the green tractor slowly move a short distance.

The remaining giant poo wall split in two. The chain gang rushed off to connect the other tractor up.

Jump arrived as two smaller poo walls were towed carefully into the factory and out of sight. An animal army was furiously brushing up the road, before washing it down to flush all traces of poo away.

The factory gates slowly closed and Jump checked out

the entrance. It was as if the giant wall of poo had never been. A rat held up a phone for him to read. 4.50. Ten seconds left.

"McGreedy! Take to the skies with all your friends. Merry Christmas to you all!"

Mr. Grumpy jumped off the coach followed by his workers. The other coaches and TV vans emptied and all followed Mr Grumpy towards the large covered thingy to the side of the main gate. In front of this was a young lady and a group of animals; Jump, Dung, Toady, Thorns and Copper stood proudly at the front. Behind them Billy, Haytor, Cuddles and a few others had stayed on for this famous moment.

Mr. Grumpy had had enough. Time to take charge again.

"What's going on here!" he shouted. The lady smiled at him.

"Merry Christmas to you too! Mr.Grumpy. Just let the reporters set their cameras up and I'll explain."
Jump looked up at Coin's keeper's identical twin sister.

Wasn't she wonderful! Oh! If only she was a squirrel monkey!

"Ladies, gentlemen, children and Team Animal. I am here to tell you that the World Plastics Factory is no more."
Mr. Grumpy gasped. His knees started shaking.
"On behalf of Team Animal I declare this new factory open!" Jane's twin sister turned to the huge covered thingy behind her.
"Giraffey! Now!" Jump hissed under his breath.
Giraffy's head appeared behind the thingy and lowering

it he got a grip on the huge blanket of interwoven banana leaves. Yummy! He slowly lifted it off the huge sign.

Billy started trumpeting. He'd read the top three giant letters.

POP

Billy loved a fizzy drink now and again. Under the letters was a huge, slowly turning globe of the world. Below that, all was explained.

'PROTECT OUR PLANET. Sustainable & Environmentally friendly Packaging Products.'

CHAPTER 6

Party Time

Back home, Billy's keeper had laid out a magical Christmas feast for them all. The huge Dung family was there, along with their many other friends.

"Did you see the look of surprise on the reporters' faces when we wished them a merry Christmas from Team Animal!" Toady said laughing.

"We did it!" Dung shouted across to a smiling, but very tired squirrel monkey.

"Go on Jump! Tell us how you made the huge poo wall disappear so quickly. It would have taken grandpa Dung a lifetime to have eaten all that!" Granny Dung asked.

Jump took a big mouthful of fresh fruit salad before slowly standing up. He was so tired.

"Oh well! If you really want to know."
Jump looked round the group of his bestest friends in the world;

Copper, Thorns, Dung and his huge family, Toady, Billy, Cuddles and Giraffey.

"Magicians really shouldn't share their tricks! The giant poo wall was hollow; constructed with a super light bamboo frame and covered in woven palm leaves.
Just cover with a bit of mud and that's it! We used real dung on the wall in front of the factory gates just to leave a pleasant smell in the air for the reporters!"

Everyone laughed.

"It was slotted together like a jigsaw and, we put it all on wheels so it could be moved quickly."

"The real magic was at the end," Dung chipped in. "After Giraffey revealed the globe sign, and Mr Grumpy and his team had been told their jobs were safe if a little different, they all noticed the huge solar panels around the factory that we'd installed and hidden under the bamboo and banana leaf covering!"

"That's what I call animal magic!" shouted a very excited grandpa Dung.

"Ho! Ho! Ho! So do I!" said an old, white bearded, red robed man who joined the group.

"I just had to drop in and say good job team animal! A very merry Christmas to you all; and thanks to you it will definitely be a happier new year for all on planet Earth. Ho! Ho! Ho!"

(Written by Zac, aged 7, & his grandpa.)

The Audiobook version of this book will be released in March 2020 on Audible, Amazon & iTunes, and will be narrated by Michael Troughton (son of Patrick Troughton – 2nd Doctor Who) the film, TV and voice actor.

Animals Save The World will return next year in:
 RAIN FORESTS EMERGENCY their new quest to help planet Earth.

PROTECT OUR PLANET

THE BLUE GYM

It is absolutely essential
To be environmental
Because it is completely
fundamental
To all our good health

So please, do go out in it
And exercise your right to it
But remember to respect,
cherish and conserve it
Just as you should with yourself

Grandpa
(Michael Ashby)
(From Pg. 42 of my Legacy poems collection paperback on
Amazon. Audiobook on Audible.)

Printed in Great Britain
by Amazon